Moonlight

Harold J. Gouveia

Contents

Chapter 1
Crazy day

☽ Aurora's pov ☽

a long day in the office and running on 2 hours of sleep and replying to emails and answering phone calls and slowly drifting off but

i get interrupted by a bang on my fucking door and suddenly i hear my door burst open followed with a loud bang

and i grab my gun and pointed it at the door to see betzy my childhood bestfriend with coffee in her hands and yells "Heyy BITCH I GOT OUR COFF-" she pauses and looks at me with the gun in my hand that is currently pointed at her and she looks at me with a smirk on her face

"Bitch i know you're ass wasn't about to shoot me like ShiT who made you mad" i slowly put the gun back in my drawer and close it and looks at betzy with a upset look and she just gives a smile

i sit back and sigh in frustration and then betzy speaks "so i have to ask you Something but promise not to get to mad"

I then look at her confused and worried bc every time she has a question it ends up going bad I sigh "what's the question this time" I sat knowing it might be something bad

"Well you know how much you love me right?"

"Yeaa why?"

"Okay so I wanted to ask if you wanted to come over to my house to have dinner and see my parents because they miss you"

"Yeaaaa no"

"Whyyy"

"Because I said no"

"My brother will be there" she says with a smirk "and plus you haven't seen him since you were little"

"wait I thought he died not gonna lie cus he disappeared for a long time"

"no he didn't your just not here when he's here"

"well shit its been like 10 something years since i lasted spoken or seen him and that was when we all used to live in Italy and i try to forget things from Italy"

i shake my head trying not to get irritated by the bad memories from my childhood

She knew what I meant by "bad memories" because she was there when most of it happened "hey look I know what happened when we were kids was traumatizing but we can't let it affect us now because we just became adults and we still have to think about the future"

i shake my head knowing she was right i couldn't fight back so i left it at that and i roll my eyes in frustration

"Fine i will go to you're house for dinner damn"

She giggled and jumped like a little girl that had to much sugar and said "ahhh thank youuuuuu your the besttttt also it's this Saturday so try not to look like a bum and dress casual okay" I nod and laugh because of the way she jokes around

"damn do i really dress like a bum like okay definitely made me feel so much better"

"Girl yes you look like a bum that scratches there asshole and smells it" I gasp by what she said "hey it's the truth I'm just being honest sometimes the truth hurts" I nod in agreement "and plus you haven't gone anywhere since you've been so busy with work and stuff" I sighed in defeat knowing she was right once again, I swear one of these day imma prove her wrong but that day won't be coming for a long time

She suddenly gets a phone call and once she's done she tells me she needs to leave and before she walks out the door she says "see you later you booty scratching T-Rex" and I flip her off as she laughs and says "I love you to" before she closes the door

i sit there and grab that ice latte that betzy got me and i take a sip of it and moan at the taste of the iced latte and sit there wondering what im going to wear Saturday since according to betzy i dress like a bum and i wonder others think that too

and i shrug it off and continue on replying to emails

hours later

i finally get home and walk upstairs and I walk in my bedroom and drop my purse on the floor and walk in my master bathroom and look at myself in the mirror looking tired as hell

walk to the shower and turn the shower on and get in and like and hour later i finally get out of the shower

i wrap the towel around my body and walk in my closet and grab some black sweatpants and a white crop top and put them on

and i realized i haven't gotten a chance to eat anything so i walk downstairs to my kitchen and make some pasta for myself

and i eat and pour myself a few glasses of champagne and wine and put some music on to set the vibe and i started feeling good

and i start dancing around like a child

til the song i was never there by the weeknd comes on

i start to sing my heart out to the song

and i stop and pause the music and check the time its 4 in morning

And then I realized I had to go to sleep even though I didn't have to go to work early tomorrow

So I decided to put my ass to sleep before I end up having no hours of sleep like I did today

Meanwhile i suddenly get woken up by my phone ringing and I answered it and said "hello" wondering who it was cus I was to tired to see who was calling

then on the other line all I hear is my bsf betzy gasping for air like she just ran a whole marathon "dude come get me like right now I think someone is following me, I'm at xxxx x xx xx" once I heard that

I got up and got my keys and ran outside to my car and started it I told her to stay on the phone with me and wait while

I was coming for her she agreed when I was only 5 mins away she suddenly said "bitch I bet this man is following me bc I'm to hot and sexy" she suddenly yells "hey pendejo ik I'm hot and all pero following me ain't Gon get you my number" and once she said that she ran and

I tried not to laugh once I turned the corner I see her running twords the car and once she gets in she yelled "DRIVE BITCH DRIVEEEE" and I hit the gas like I was in fast and furious

Once we get to my house she went to my room and changed into some clothes cus she has some of her stuff at my house once she's done changing she jumps in my bed and says "goodnight booty scratching T-Rex" I laugh knowing I had to deal with this ever since I was little, I get into bed and go to sleep

(The end of chapter one)

(if there grammar mistakes don't come for me or ima shove a stick up ur ass)

SEE YOU LOVES IN THE NEXR CHAPTER;)

Chapter 2

business event

☽ Aurora's pov ☽

i wake up to what felt like a train running over my head hangover

i started to toss back and forth in the bed i grab my pillow and put it on top of my head and i take the pillow off my face and look and see no sign of betzy next to me

Oh SHIT WHERE THE FUCK IS SHE AT

i get up and jog down the stairs and run all around my house trying to look for her

then i realized I haven't check the kitchen im such a dumbass

i walking quietly towards the big luxurious kitchen to see betzy cooking that smells absolutely delicious

i knew i could trust her when it comes to cooking her mom taught us ever since we were little

i consider her mom Guadalupe like a other mom because betzy parents helped alot with raising me

her father lioñel was the good father i wish i had

he actually got me out of the toxic household i used to live in with my dad and three other siblings

i really appreciated betzy and her parents for being there for me

but my mother on the other hand she found someone else and left me and my siblings to suffer

but recently she found my company and came begging for me to forgive her and i practically her kicked out of my life

just how she kicked me out of her life

my father ran the Mexican mafia and all he cared about was who was gonna run his empire for when he dies

but sadly he passed away due to alcohol poisoning or alcohol overdose

like 7 years ago

but my older sister zella took the responsibility to take over my father's mafia because she knew i wasn't up for the offer which was nice of her to do

my father never really cared for me or my siblings

it was all about his mafia and alcohol and sex to him but never his family

but that wasn't going to affect me and my siblings life well at least it still didn't affect my siblings probably just me but just a little bit

but here i am staring at my bestfriend betzy cooking her swaying her body to the music

then she looks up and sees me and smiles and i give her a smile back in return and i walk back upstairs and get ready for this event i had to go to today which requires wearing a dress

but i hate wearing dresses because of the catcalls usually because it's the old creepy men who do it or sometimes be touchy to the point where i don't know what to do

i approach the bathroom and walk in and look at myself in the mirror and frown in disgust

and i open the cabinet and grab my face wash and turn the sink on.....wash my face

i dry my face with a clean towel and walk to my closet and grab the beautiful red dress

The dress

i start to think maybe this might look good for the occasion so i walk to the bathroom and remove my clothes and put the beautiful red dress on

i turn to the mirror and frown again in disappointment thinking it would've looked good on me

well it's whatever

i applie light makeup on my face which only took maybe 15 minutes to do

i finally get done with that and start to curl my hair

which took 30 minutes to do

and i get done doing that and run to my clothes and grabs my ysl heels and putting them on and walking down stairs

and grab my car keys and walking passed the living where betzy was and she looks at me and screaming "AWW YOU LOOK SO BEAUTIFUL MY LOVE" she yells in a high pitched voice

"aww thanks you but i need to get going you can use one of the cars if you need to" she gives that eyes and speaks

"Auroraa where the fuck are you going dressed like that foorr huh?"

betzy saids with a curious tone and look on her face

i say

"uhhh i have a work event to go to whyy"

"Because i don't want no fucking creep to look at my Hot very Sexy bestfriend of mine you got a problem with that Huh"

betzy saids practically yelling at me

"Why are you yelling at me for shit" i say annoyed as hell

"Because you got me pissed now got to you're little event you Have To Go TO BYE LOVE YOUU" betzy saids and continues to watching TV

"BYEE LOVE YOU TOO"

and walk to my garage and get into my car and speed off to the event

as i approached the huge luxurious building i park

and walk towards the entrance of the building and one of thebody-guards ask

"can i get a name please ma'am"

the bodyguard ask

"Aurora Selén kñight"

the guard looks at the clipboard in his hands and nods and points at the door entrance and i walk into the beautiful luxurious building i admire the beautiful lobby and walk in the main room full of people and tables and some gambling and all types of stuff

i start walking past the crowd of people

and i see lorenzo one of my good high school friends who is a ceo of a clothing and a few other companies

i wave him down and he turns his head and spots me and smiles and walks towards me

and approaches me "oh well look who decided to show up" lorenzo teases he grabs my hand brings it up to lips to peck it gently and lets go slowly and looks down at me

"don't you think that dress is a little too short for you" Lorenzo saids with one of his eyebrows arched

don't get me wrong he is extremely good looking and the way looked at me was just wow

"yeah i know it something that was quick and ready to go and is totally not that good on me" i say

lorenzo gasps at what i said What did i say wrong oh my god

"aurora please never say that bullshit like ever again you are fucking gorgeous and this sexy little dress on you looks sexy you know how many men in here who are willing to rip this dress of you please don't say that mk"

lorenzo saids in my ear

i stay frozen at his words and lorenzo backs away and stares at me up and down grabs my hand again and gives it one more kiss and said

"well have a wonderful night hermosa will see you soon" he walks away never in a thousand years would i think lorenzo Sanchez would ever say that to me oh my fucking God

i slowly walk to the table of more of the mutual friends and take a sit and say hi to everyone

then a few minutes later the top 3 most best CEOs will be called out

"Hello everyone today we are here to celebrate the day were we call out the best CEOs for there good work and donations for those in need"

everyone starts clapping then stops so the lady can call out the names

"in Top numbers three we have someone who has Sent 30 Million dollars to the homeless shelter and have 15 companies and thats is, Anthony Walker moore"

everyone claps for him

he walks up and does his stupid ass speech and walks back to his table

now its time to see who taking second place

"now we have someone who has donated 50 million dollars to families in need owns 17 companies and at second place we have.. ..lorenzo de luca Sanchez"

he walks up and does his speech and walks back to his table

and then the lady speaks again

"now we have the best for last the person we donated 100 million dollars to the children cancer's center and owns 25 companies we have the one and only"

"Aurora Selén Kñight"

i look around in shocked not expecting it to be me and I get up as i walk up to the stage people clapping their hands and laughter

it was a once a year event and i only won 3 rewards my whole career

i walk up to the microphone and look at the happy crowd staring at me waiting for me to talk

"well hello everyone i just wanna come here tonight and say how much i appreciate all the love and support that all those who were counting on me and if it wasn't for you lovely people i wouldn't be here to day but anyways i have everyone has an amazing night"

i say my speech and walks off the stage and i walk down the mini stairs and i see lorenzo holding his hand out and i put my hand on his and he helps me get down

"congratulations hermosa you earned it, I'm proud of you hermosa"

he saids leaning close to my ear and his hot breath hits my neck and instant chills form on my body

"t-thank you mr.Sanchez"

i say stuttering

"well see you soon hermosa"

lorenzo saids and walks away

what a Friday night for me i finally get home to a empty house and i take a shower and changed

go to bed

heyy loves hoped you enjoyed it see you later:))

Chapter 3
confusion

□

□mauricio pov□

sitting down in my office in my house after getting back from one of my warehouses after some little gang left a message on the way out leaving one of my men drowning in his own blood dead

finding out that someone is dead is nothing to me knowing i grew up seeing shit like this but it's whatever

i sigh in frustration knowing i have paper work to do but I'll deal with it later

i just have to sign one paper and I'll handle the rest for later

as i grab a pen someone storms into my office door my eyes shoot up to see my crazy ass little sister betzy

what the hell does she want from me now!!

i get slightly annoyed at the fact she just opened and slammed my door all crazy

she smiles and looks around and her eyes to towards me

"heyyyy my dear brotherrrrr you look soooo good today" betzy saids with a smirk on her face

"What the fuck do you want"i say trying to stay patient with her

"Ohhh nothinggggg"

she's fucking lying there's always something!!!

"You better tell me right now or ima tell mom what you did" I said with a straight face

"Fineeeee geezzzz" betzy whines

"You need to hurry because I have somewhere to be" I told her " soooo remember Aurora?" She asks

"Yea why...bitch what the fuck did you do this time" say with a serious look on my face

"Well~ she may or may not be coming to dinner with us this weekend" she said with her eyes closed

the fuck...?

"oh my lord why the fuck didn't you tell me sooner" i said

" hey I just got and answer from her like 3 hrs ago chill out you big bafoon" she said as she rolled her eyes

Like always!!!

i sit there staring at her with a blank expression on my face not knowing what to say at that

"Wait remind me who that is again" i say being kinda confused on who it was, all i know is the name but it was the name that sorta ringed a bell but couldn't remember her

"you know what never mind you'll find out when you see her this weekend" betzy saids

I sighed wondering who she was talking About because there's no way she talking about the Aurora we used to hangout with when we were younger i guess I'll have to wait and see for myself on who Aurora is........

betzy casually walks away and out of my office

i let out a big sigh and spin my chair around to my window and stare at the beautiful view of the city

i get up and walk to the little bar area that i have in my office

and i grab a glass cup and scoop up a few peices of ice in my glass and pour some whiskey into my glass and slowly a sip of it

i slowly walk back to the window and stand there and admire the view once again

the i hear a present behind me and i see my father standing next to me also with a glass of whiskeyin his hand

"well hello dad how are you doing" i ask my father

"I'm doing fine son but how are you doing" my father ask i take another sip

"I'm doing okay i guess just been very busy but tomorrow im off i have Diego taking care of it" i tell my father who was smirking

I Knew that look He's gonna DO SOMETHING AWW SHIT

"Dad why the fuck are you smirking for" i tell my father a curious tone

my father starts to laugh "nothing just wait for til Saturday i have a offer for you" my father saids evil tone in his voice

"uhh okay" then right as i was about to speak he speaks up

"well i must get back to mama before she tries to kill me and cuss me out but have a wonderful night see you Saturday for the dinner" my father saids and walks out i watch him walk out then i sit back down on my office chair and start to drink again

and play some music.......

10 drinks later

the perfect song comes on by the weeknd wicked games

i close my eyes and hum to the song and throw my head back

then my sister betzy yells

"Mauricio kingston caraliño whyy the fuck are you drinking this much c'mon let's go to sleep"

i whine at her

"NOoooo leave me the fuck alone im trying to sleep"

then i feel a hard ass slap on my face

"WAKE THE FUCK UP DUMBASS BITCH" betzy yells once again

"SHIT Fine I'll get up FUck" i complain and get up and push her tiny ass out of my way

"yes big bitch ass walk you're ass to you're bed as you should" betzy saids with attitude

i turn to look at her and give her a serious look and she just smiles

psycho ass

then i turn and continue to walk back to my bedroom

and betzy continues to walk next to me

"so why do you want me to go to dinner so badly betzy" i ask as i roll my eyes and let out a sigh

then she didn't hesitate to say why

"Oohhh just because Brrottherrr"

betzy saids with her lying ass

"whatever" i say as i approach my bedroom and turn to look at betzy "well goodnight princess I'll see you Saturday and please be safe and if you need me give me a call okay" i tell her

she nods her head yes

and she walks away and i close my bedroom door and walk to tye balcony

and stand by the railing and stare at the moon and stars with the cool breeze of the wind

i run my hand through my fluffy black hair

and the dark memories hit me

the night where we were in Italy and the night i heard my mom telling my dad goodbye

and to figure out my dad left to become the mafia leader that i am today for my father

just remember my little betzy crying begging for our father to return back home was like hell for me and my mother

i had to take very good care of betzy because my mother was also a very busy woman

but one day i turned 17 and all i remember was a black car pulled up by our house and a familiar tall man with just the same features as me

Black hair, very tall, those very stunning green eyes,

and that's when it all hit me my father was back but why now

he left without saying goodbye to me and betzy

he looked nice but he looked different

he had a bunch of tattoos bunch of rings on his fingers

he walked up to the doorstep and knocked i seen my mom open the door not looking super surprised

like she knew he was coming back

i couldn't let betzy see him betzy started to grow hating him for the way he left without a warning but before i could make it to her bedroom she already seen him

she stood there with no emotion on her face but in her eyes there was anger and pain there

i knew when she was hurt mentally and physically

but damn the cold look on her face said everything she wasn't happy to see him

it was like her eye's were talking

or i should say throwing knives at him

my father stood there looking into her eyes

my father didn't dare to look at her eye's in any wrong way

and the worst part was our mother didn't get in her or hisway

she just stood by our father and followed his lead

and i could see in my father's eyes there was

reget, guilt, pain, and something that i couldn't quite figure out

and then he looked at me and a little smile grew on his face

"hello son how are you"

end of flashback

i snap out of my thoughts and walk back inside and take a shower and head to bed tired well at least i don't work for a few days

hello loves thanks for reading CHAPTER Three hoped you enjoyed reading it

see ya next CHAPTER

Chapter 4

Dinner

⊹ Aurora's pov⊹

i wake up and rub my eyes that were still trying to stay shut

i finally am able to open my eyes and i look to my left and look at the clock on my nightstand

to see that its 3:37 in the afternoon....WHAT THE FUCK

it's Saturday

i get up and walk down stairs and make me my lunch and eat

i would usually at this time be out doing something

i hear my phone buzz and i walk to the kitchen counter and grab it

to only see who it was and it was lioñel that texted me

Lioñel

HEY AURORA ARE YOU STILL COMING TO DINNER AT 6 TONIGHT Sweetheart

AURORA

HEY im so sorry i forgot all about dinner tonight but I'm still coming to dinner tonight

Lioñel

oh sweetheart there is nothing to be sorry about you're a very busy young woman and you have a lot on you're plate but see you tonight and make good decisions

AURORA

I always doand see you tonight

i sit my phone down and walk upstairs and start getting ready for dinner later i had no clue what to wear for this dinner

and betzy said dress good for this dinner like what the hell why i always dress good

she's so mean to me but i love her

i finally find a beautiful black dress

i took a shower and did my makeup and curled my hair

and put the dress on and i still am not impressed with the dress even with a hourglass body i still feel werid in it

The dress

her hair

i walk down stairs and grab my keys and check the time and it was 5:40

i sprint towards the front door and run out the house and run to my car and getting in and speeding away

15 minutes later

i make it to the caraliño house

and i get out the car and slowly approach the doorstep i ring the door bell and see Lioñel who opened the door and greeted me with a smile and a bear hug he pointed at the hallway where betzy bedroom was so i walked to her room and see betzy laying on her side on her phone in this

she screams "ahhh you made it yayy!" i stand there with a embarrassed look on my face

and she frowns at me and scans my whole body with her eyes

"Aurora you loook so sexy just wait til mauric-" she stops herself from finishing her sentence

and i look at her with a serious look on my face and walk away from her and out of her room and walk into the dining room and I see a very tall man with black hair, beautiful yet intimidating green eyes, with rings on his fingers, tattoos, and was very gorgeous, with a black dress shirt and black slacks

but i hear betzy who was standing next to me smirking and so was Lioñel and Guadalupe who was sitting down looking guilty of something she wouldn't look at me or anyone there

"Well aurora this is mauricio my son you might remember him from Italy when you were children" i keep a straight face and shake his hand and he shakes my hand gently

and we walk to our seats and i sit next to betzy and right across from mauricio and another man walks in and looked good himself and another came in aswell

they both said hi to everyone and then they stop and look at me

and the one with black hair said "hello my name is Ace and you"

"hi my name is Aurora" then his face goes in shock and

he clears his throat and speaks up again "wait um aren't you like one the most successful CEOS in America" i nod my head to his question then the other guy with dark brown hair who looked so fucking familiar introduces himself "well hello Aurora my name is Alex" that's when it hit me he was my ex from years back

ahh whatever

i turn to look at betzy but she was zoned out so i look at Guadalupe who was also zoned out

now everything got werid quickly

and i just look at my lap and stare and zoned out

lioñel clears his thoat that grabs everyone's attention

"well now to the offer i have given you" lioñel looks at me "and you mauricio" he looks at mauricio and i look at lioñel confused and as i was about to speak up i get cut off

"ill go get the papers stay put"

and he gets up and walks away into the very dim hallway

i started to panic so i stand up about to walk out til i hear a voice

"Sit back down Aurora" i snap my head back to who said that to only see mauricio who was staring at me with a serious look on his face

i sit back down and start feeling overwhelmed trying to take control of my breathing

i look at betzy who was sitting there looking guilty and Guadalupe was staring at her plate of food

and lioñel comes back with a paper and sat back in his seat and slide the paper towards us

and me and mauricio look at it and we get confused on why it said contract we look at lioñel waiting for him to explain it "okay well how about we walk to my office and I'll explain more"

we nod our heads and get up and follow lioñel to his office and we walk into the dim hallway and we approach his office and walk in and we take a seat

lioñel sits down and looks at the paper and smirk at it

"okay well I'll just get to the point Aurora you're company is big and all and mauricio you have a biggest mafia in the world and the reason i have the two of you here is because i need y'all to get married because number one i want grandchildren and number two it's makes this family a stronger empire than it already is and number three yall two look amazing together"

my heart dropped i felt sick to my stomach

i am able maintain my calm

"dad are you fucking joking right now" mauricio saids in a calm tone lioñel shakes his head no

i stay quiet i start bouncing my legs

"mr. caraliño i don't want this"i tell lioñel he looks at me with no emotion on his face

"well this isn't you're choice it's his" lioñel saids while looking at mauricio

when i turn my head to look at mauricio

he speaks up

"but what if i don't want to marry her mhm?" maurico saids with a what seemed like a sarcastic tone in his voice

asshole!!

i start hoping that mauricio would knock some sense into his own father from trying to get us to marry each other

"and plus dad I'm too young and i have more important things to do than be marry to ms. knight seriously" mauricio saids with a rude ass tone

what a rude ass bitch

and how the fuck does he know my last name i snap out of my thoughts

"son you are damn near 30 that's not young and it's either you marry her or I'll kill you're bestfriend and trust me son i will" lioñel saids with a smirk on his face

"but dad she's like a damn child compared to me and you can't do this that's being selfish of you"mauricio saids

i gasp at how he called me a child Mauricio looks at me and smirks and lets out a sigh

"Fine give me the contract" Mauricio saids with a annoyed tone

i shake my head trying to not to show any emotion but my anxiety attack start to develop

my breathing start getting fasteonly short breaths could hardly breathe much i could feel my heart beating out of my chest

i started to shake i see Mauricio starring at me after signing the contract and so did lioñel

lioñel yells out for Guadalupe and betzy to rush over here

betzy comes running bursting into the room and running towards me and helps me get up as we walk out of lioñels office we go to betzy's room and I sit there not saying much just staying mouth shut

"I'll be right back i have to use the bathroom" i say getting up and walking in the hallway i walk into the bathroom and close the door behind me

i look at myself in the mirror looking at my smudged mascara from crying

i grab one of betzy's makeup removers and

remove all the makeup from my face

and i walk out of the bathroom and walk in betzy's room

"hey can i borrow some pajama pants from you and a top please"

i ask betzy and she gasps and looks at me dumbfounde

"what the fuck kind of question is that of course you can there in my closet to the left" she points at the closet

"t-thank you" i tell her she smiles and nods her head

i walk in to the closet and change out of the dress

and into a black crop top and pajama pants

and i excused myself to the bathroom and walk into the hallway and walk quietly to the

front door trying to leave without anyone noticing i open the door and walk out quietly and smoothly and i walk to my car thinking i got free

til i hear a present behind me and i look to see mauricio leaning against him car

i act like i didn't see him

"where you headed off to princess mhm?"

Mauricio calls out and i stop and turn to look at him
"im headed home Mauricio why"i say out loud with a attitude
"well damn" he saids and walks over to me
but what happens after that
wait and see in the next chapter
(THANK YOU LOVES)

Chapter 5

im not yours

Recap aurora said she was going to the bathroom but really try to sneak out of the caraliño house but Mauricio caught her and is now walking towards her

AURORA'S POV

Mauricio starts walking towards me and Approaches me and looks me up and down

"sheesh well i can't know where my wife is going hmm" Mauricio saids sarcastically

"im not you're wife Mauricio" i say annoyed

"that's not what the contract saids and you're not leaving if that's what you think" Mauricio saids and it went to him being sarcastic to being serious

i look at Mauricio with a serious look on my face

"Mauricio you have no control on where i can and cannot go you're not my dad you asshole" i yell out loud at Mauricio

and i try to open my car door just so it could be slammed back shut "oh miss knight trust me i get to control what's mine" Mauricio saids having me leaning against my car on my stomach feeling his warm breath hit my neck with him right behind me

i stay quiet

"now i would suggest you're ass come get in my car and let's go get something to eat and catch up on some things" Mauricio saids while pointing at his dark grey matte colored Ferrari

i walk to his car and i walk to it and get in the passenger seat

and he gets in the driver seat and he starts driving

it stays quiet for a few minutes then he takes a deep breath

"so why did you and my friend alex have this werid vibe once he walked in and introduced himself to you" Mauricio saids having one hand on the steering wheel and the other on the console

"that's only for me to know and for you to stay out of" i tell mauricio

he chuckles while shaking his head

"well i don't care whether it's my business or not i asked why was the vibe werid between the two of you" Mauricio saids with no emotion on his face

"i will maybe when i can trust you enough" i tell Mauricio

he chuckles once again

"ha so funny Aurora" Mauricio saids with a annoyed tone

"yeah Ookay MAUrIcIO" i say making fun of his name

"don't say my name like that like ever again" Mauricio saids "but why not that's how you say it isn't" i ask mauricio "yeah..No you made fucking fun of my name but saying it all dumb" Mauricio saids while focusing on the road

"yeah what a werid name for a werid man" i say while turning my head to look at the window

"hmm...you're lucky you are my little sister's bestfriend and my wife because if you weren't you would have been dead a long time ago" Mauricio saids with a serious tone in his voice

that scared me knowing he could kill me any second he wanted too

i just stay quiet and look out the window

there was the awkward silence the whole car ride

til i look up and see were at ihop and he parks the car into the empty parking lot with only a few cars parked in it

i open the door and get out and start walking towards the entrance and beat Mauricio inside the restaurant

i stand there waiting for Mauricio who was taking his sweet ass time walking inside

i roll my eyes at him and he flips me off

Asshole

he walks up beside me

"a table for two please" Mauricio saids nicely

that's Hot.....yeah ima just shut the fuck up

"table or booth sir" the lady asks nicely with a smile

"a Booth please" Mauricio ask and the lady nods her head and grabs two menu's and starts walking in front of us and we follow her

til she makes a stop and sets the menu's down on the table for us

she pointed at the table to let us know that we can sit down i sit down and Mauricio sits across from me

i grab the menu and started looking for something to get

but i could feel Mauricio eyes on me making me slightly uncomfortable then after a few minutes he finally stops staring at me and starts looking at the menu

"how long have you been in texas for or America Ethier way" mauricio saids very calmly

"for a few years" i say very dry and fast

"by yourself...?" i look at Mauricio and roll my eyes

"no mauricio..." i say annoyed by his questions

"why are you getting all riled up for im just asking you stuff"

"Mauricio i don't care" i tell him as i try to calm myself down a bit

"well i don't care either Aurora i just haven't seen you in years" Mauricio saids leans against the table and staring at me

i grab the menu trying to block his view

and him pushing the menu down and my hands going down with it

"and how the fuck did you manage to get into America without being caught Aurora...huh?"

i look at him and look at him up in down and hum

"Mauricio i could ask you the same damn thing so get the fuck out of my face if you are not willing to explain"

Mauricio smirks and stays still

"Aurora you don't know what you are dealing with now fucking tell me how do you get into America" he saids grabbing my wrist aggressive he held a very tight grip on to my wrist that i tried not to cry show now emotion

he gets up and grabs me all crazy and leads me out the diner

we finally make it to the parking lot and he slams my back hard on to the car

a sharp pain hits my back and i couldn't help my eyes from tearing up

i tried to keep my tears in my eyes and trying to not let them fall

"so are you going to tell me" he yells while still griping on both of my wrist very hard

i start to have flashbacks of when from my childhood

i just look at mauricio "please stop you are hurting me" i cry out loud

he looks at me with a shocking look on his face as he let's go of me

he backs away and i start walking away and walking towards the sidewalk

"Aurora get the fuck back over here" Mauricio yells out loud

i ignore him and keep walking and as time went by i finally approached

a bar that i been going to for while now its like family there

i walk in and i see shelly one of the bartender's and bill the owner

i walk towards the bar "hello guys" i say quietly

"heyy Aurora" shelly and bill both say

it was slow at this time at night only a few groups of people here

"so what can i get ya tonight miss Aurora" shelly asks

"give me a Budweiser" i tell shelly who was standing there with her hand on her hip

"aurora there is no way in hell you are ordering a Budweiser" shelly tells me

"yeah i know right couldn't see myself ordering that either" i saying with a smile on my face

"okay Aurora what ever you say its coming right up" shelly saids walking away

and i feel someone walking up to me

"well it's crazy to see a CEO out in some bar like this all by herself"

i look to see who said that and see a gorgeous man standing beside me

"you look familiar how do i know you" i tell the man "well im Mauricio's bestfriend but my name is Ace"

"oohh hey Ace uhh how are you" i ask him with a small smile and other person comes behind him and pushes him out of the way

his hair was dark brown and had dark brown eyes tall with tattoos as well and very handsome

"Well hello Darling" the other familiar man saids with his hand out encouraging me to shake it

i reach my hand out and he kisses it i slightly blush

"so what's got you out here tonight all alone" Ace ask with a curious look on his face

"mhm i don't know really just one of those nights i guess" i tell him while his friend stands right beside him

"well it's not safe for a beautiful woman like you to be out here alone at night" his friend saids

WHO THE FUCK IS HE

"Uhh what's you're name again" i ask the guy with the dark brown hair

he chuckles and shakes his head and looks back at me "Alex my name is ALEX"

OHH SHIT!

NOT HIM...!!!!

"uh oh okay" i say taking a drink of the beer bottle in my hand

i get a call from Betzy

i answer it

"heyy AURORAAA!!!" Betzy yells through the phone

"heyy betzyy?" i say back betzy speaks up again

"where the fuck are you i literally hear music in the background"betzy saids not so happy with me

"im at a bar Bezty....." i sing

"okay bet ima pull up on you shawty" betzy saids with a bad manly voice

i laugh as the line went dead

i put my phone down and continue to drink my beer

after 10 minutes i hear someone walk into the bar

and i turn the spinny stool around to see who it was

and it was my love BETZY......

she comes running towards me and giving me a tight bear hug

and god she smelled amazing as always

she is so beautiful to me

"hii Aurora" betzy saids with a smile

"hii betzyy" i say back i wait for her to order her drink and she starts talking about a guy shes been crushing on lately

and i try to be there for her as much as possible because she been there for me forever

she's like my little sister and i will always have to protect

then she stops talking and looks at me

"hey Aurora you good talk to me what's wrong" betzy saidscon-cerned

"uhh please don't get mad at me" i tell her

"Aurora im not gonna get mad at you what's wrong" betzy reas-sures me

"well Mauricio just put his hands on me for not telling him how i got into America" i say looking down and my beer bottle

betzy tries not a let her anger out in public so she shakes her head and slams her drink down her throat

sorry but DAMN WHAT A DEEP THOAT....yea wrong time

"When was this Aurora" betzy saids with a serious look on her face

"like maybe 1 hour ago" i tell her

"Mhmm okayy Aurora well I'll talk with him about that" betzy with a smirk on her face

uuhhh okayy that's suspicious that's werid

betzy leaves and here i am after

a few shots and beer drunk as hell

"okayy lets get you home" some guy saids

oohh he saids hot as fuckk!!

i feel someone pick me up but i don't know by who tho..???

i feel that im now sitting back on a comfy chair

and i hear a car door shut and i few minutes later i hear the car door open and i feel two strong arms

pick me up bridal style carry

GOD WHO IS THISS????

eventually i get put down and now i could tell im on a bed

NOT MY BED FOR SSUreee

but sooo comfy more comfy than my bed the blanket smell like expensive cologne

SMELLS SOO GOOOD!!!

i couldn't see anything im too too drunk right now

my eyes are shut

right when im about to fall asleep i hear the anonymous man say something

"God I'm so sorry mi amor i will never hurt you again" the man saids while brushing the hair off from my face

then i fell asleep

---

hey loves i hope y'all enjoyed this chapter but i will try and post another chapter today

but what do y'all think about this chapter

who's you're favorite character

BETZY

AURORA

ACE

ALEX

MAURICIO

Y'ALL LET ME KNOW

HAVE A WONDERFUL DAY AND DRINK WATERR:)))

BYEEE:)))

Chapter 6
everywhere

Mauricio pov

after i found Aurora drunk at a bar where my bestfriends were at

Ace called me and told me Aurora was drunk at our hang out spot

i went and got her i saw her dancing with Fucking Alex

i hated the fact he was touching her like if they had history together

which they probably do but still and didn't respect it because Alex knows

about the arranged marriage and for him to look at her and touch her pisses me off

but when i walked in he's holding her hips and shes just her i wasn't mad at her but i was mostly mad at him i wanted to walk over there and beat the living shit out of him

but god damn she is fucking gorgeous but a side of guilt hits me

i hated to admit it but i always loved her even though she's 9 years younger then me i don't care

i have always loved her and the fucking look on her face when i hit her back against my car i hate that i scared her and shit i was mostly scared that she would tell my little sister because if betzy were to find out

im dead meat there's no savings me from that evil ass girl

"heyy man" alex saids i look at him with anger in my eyes

he lets go of Aurora and she's very fucking drunk god damn

i pick her up bridal style and carry her to my car

i sit her inside the passenger seat and buckle her in and closed the door and walk to the other side to the driver side

i get in and start driving and after 20 minutes of driving i pull up to my house

and get out and walk to the other side of the car and i pick up Aurora bridal style into my house

i walk upstairs with her in my arms

shes so fucking tiny

i finally approach my bedroom and lay her down on the bed

i put the covers on top of her body

i watch her cuddle the covers which was actually kinda cute

i brush the hair from her face behind her ear

"god I'm so sorry mi amor i will never hurt you again" i say softly

i get up and i go take a shower and go to bed

8 hours later.

i managed to wake up before Aurora and do some mafia work in my office in my house

and i honestly still wanted to sleep but aurora was still dead asleep in my room so i just let her be

til i hear someone scream

"WHERE THE FUCK AM I" i hear Aurora scream out loud

i walk over to my room and see Aurora sitting up on my bed her tired eyes

"Aurora you got drunk last night and Alex almost took you with him so i saved you in a way" i say calmly with my hands in my pockets of my sweatpants

she rolls her eyes and takes the covers off her and gets up and runs her hand through her curly i guess wavy hair

she starts walking towards me and stops about 1 feet away from me

"well thank you but how much do i owe you" Aurora saids with a curious tone in her voice

"Aurora you don't owe me a dime at all" i tell her, she tilts her head sideways

"Mauricio come on-" i didn't let her finish her sentence

"im not gonna argue with you about money señorita" i tell heras i look down at her

her trying to reach into her purse i stop her by grabbing the purse from her

"Auroraaa" i sing and she look up at me with a smile

"Mauricio give me back my purse and not leaving til i pay you" Aurora whines

"I don't care i already told you i don't want you to pay me" tell her

she sighs in frustration

"and plus Aurora i owe you for last night before the bar situation" i tell her "oh..." Aurora saids looking awayi could see her rethinking about it and her not wanting to look at me

"i just wanna say I'm sorry for putting my hands on you i was angry i guess" i say look down at her who is just staring down at the floor

"it's okay it's nothing new to me" Aurora saids with no emotion in her voice

it was cold how she said it

"Aurora what do you mean by that" i say concerned

and sighs and looks back up at me "it's nothing but i must get going i got things to do" Aurora saids like she didn't something off at all

and she walks away and i turn and watch her walk down the stairs

and i walk into the hallway and walk to the railing by the stairs and see Aurora walk to the front door and open it

but before she walks out she stops and looks back at me with a smile

"Thanks you Mauricio take good care" Aurora saids with that beautiful smile of her

and walks out and closes the door gently

damn what a respectful young woman she is

i start walking back into my office and keep working

til a few hours later i get a phone call from betzy and i pick up and all i hear is betzy going off on me

"Mauricio Kingston caraliño im going to fucking murder you for what you did to aurora last night mhm yea didn't think of i wouldn't find out well bitch i always find out so when i see you i swear to gawd ima going to shove my foot up your ass" Betzy said screaming into the phone and talking so fucking fast but to the point where I could hear everything she just said

"betzy calm the fuck down" i say

"no stupid bitch just fucking wait Mauricio im torture you STUPID ASS BITCH" betzy saids yelling at me

and the line went dead she hung up

Oh noo Aurora fucking told her

im soo dead!!!.....

Aurora's pov

after i left Mauricio's house i went home and packed some clothes and skincare products and some of my perfumes and makeup

because I'm taking some time to myself after all the work i have been doing

but i have to hurry and get to my private jet so i can go to paris for maybe a week or two

really depends knowing that my company's always need me for stuff

but it's okay even if it's for 3 days it fine i can always come back another time

but i finally get down packing and have my body guards help me get my stuff into the car

and we were on the road and after 30 minutes of a drive

we finally arrive to my private jet

before i get out of the car i recieve a message from betzy

B: hey aurora i talked to my brother everything is fine

okay that's good but I'll text you later:A

and i turned my phone off and got out of the car and went on my jet and fell asleep

after hours later we have finally arrived to paris

it's so beautiful to me

i get the nicest hotel in paris that had the best view of the Eiffel Tower

i walked in the hotel and set some of my bags down and jumped onto the comfy king size bed

i just laid there for a few minutes looking outside the window staring at the Eiffel Tower that was just beautiful

i sigh at the fact that im always business and i never see my sisters

my brother not so much he's the asshole who tried to kill us for the mafia that wasn't given to him

but it honestly didn't matter who got it or not

because in the end of the day weare pretty bad people for what we have done to other's

because we wanted our father to be proud but nothing ever worked his just became worse

and especially after my mom left my dad he became someone we didn't really know

and we treated us like his slave's and didn't know why he did do the things he did to us

but for some oddly reason why did he want me to have the mafia out of my older sister and my older brother

what was special about me anyways

but i especially remember when my dad beat me so bad i managed to get to betzy's house

her father lioñel opened the door and was shocked at my condition

i was all bloody i had bruises, cuts and couldn't feel anything

but lioñel took me and my sister's out of the situation and let us stay with them for as long as we wanted to

my brother was oldest so he never really experienced any abuse in his life because he's was spoiled

but i grew close to Mauricio a little bit

i remember i would wake up at night and get a glass of water

and Mauricio would be awake and he would ask me if i wanted to hear him play his electric guitar and i would say yes

and there was a few times i would fall asleep listening to him play and would wake up to him holding me

he was such an angel to me and he would treat me like a princess

but here i am someone who is a millionaire and is the betzy CEO of America

but anyways i took a shower and went to bed

but i kinda understood why Mauricio got upset with me

i could see he was worried and was curious and concerned about the situation from years ago

but it is what it is what can we do nothing just have to live with it and move forward with our lives______________________________

(heyy loves hope you enjoyed)

but how do you feel about this chapter

but sorry i haven't posted a chapter in a few days i just been busy with life stuff

but i wil try and make and post chapter as fast as possible

but byee love yall<33

Chapter 7

Surprised

(Please don't be a silent reader)

betzy's pov:

i was in shock to find out Mauricio did that to Aurora

i honestly didn't want to believe it but i knew Aurora wasn't lying to me and that's the part that broke me into a million pieces

i always loved Aurora as a big sister and i looked up to her

she was always so sweet, chilled and laid back and was stunning, and very understanding and had a good body, and smart,and a survivor

but i do feel like if Mauricio knew about her past he would've handled himself better

because Mauricio and i both don't stand by abuse or rape and other sexual violence

but how could Mauricio do that to her she's so innocent

after i went off on Mauricio i sat there for a minute trying to process everything going on in my life

but i get a text from kai

it was a guy I've liked for quite some time and he's so sweet to me but he literally hates everyone but treats me like a princess

Kaihey hermosa

Betzyhey kaiii!!!

Kaiwhat are you doing right now?

Betzy mhm nothing just at home and you?

Kai mhm nothing also just wondering if you want to go get something to eat with me

Betzyi would love that when tho?

Kai well i was thinking i could come pick you up right now

Betzy mhmm okay i guess I'll see you then

---

i got ready and i went to my closet and grabbed some ripped jeans and a graphic t shirt

and put on my shoes

and fixed my makeup a little bit

after he picked me up we went to a fancy restaurant and we sat down and started looking at our menu's

til kai broke the silence "so how was you're day amor" kai said while staring at me with his gorgeous brown eyes

"it was good just had a lot going on that's all tho" i tell him and he nods his head gently

"do you wanna talk about it hermosa?" kai saids with a concern look on his face and his eyes softened

"well it's a lot to hear" i tell him

"baby don't worry I'm not going anywhere tell me what's wrong"kai saids putting his hand on top of mine

"i guess if you insist then okay" i say to him

"so what's going on princess" kai saids waiting for me to speak

"well you know my bestfriend Aurora right?" i ask him

"yeah that one girl who cussed out one of my friends..yea i remember her" he saids while laughing

gawd damn his smile is to die for

"well my older brother and her are in a arranged marriage and my father forced it on both of them" i tell kai

"ohh shitt...." kai saids with a shocking look on his face

"yea its crazy but Mauricio put hands on her and she told me" i also tell him

"do you know why he did that to her or...?" kai saids

i pause trying to not imagine the Aurora getting her by my own blood

"well she didn't say what he exactly did but she ended up showing me the bruise on her back" i say quietly

kai remains silent and looks around and so do i

"but i thought you're brother and you don't stand by abuse..?" kai said

"that's so i thought but i guess not" i say frustrated

"look let's just eat our food and enjoy our time togetherbeautiful" kai saids with a smile

that showed his dimples

i just nod my head and we eat and talk about random things

after we had dinner he dropped me off at home and i started to get comfortable

i put on some pajamas pants on and a tshirt

and i figured i should give Aurora a call she i went on my phone and looked for her name in my contacts

and i found it and called her

ring ring*ring*ring*

i hear someone pick it up and i hear that one calming soft soothing voice answered the phone

"hello?" Aurora saids and it sounds a little windy where she was at

"hii Auroraa where you right now" i ask her

"im in paris sitting on a balcony of the best view...whyy" Aurora saids happily

"and why the fuck are you in paris....?? are you alone" i say

"well i mean why not betzy" Aurora saids trying to be a smart ass

"Aurora i swear to fucking god if you are all alone in Paris i won't hesitate to bring my ass over there" i go off on her

"geez betzy it's alright nothing bad is gonna happen to me and seriously what's the worst that can happen" Aurora saids

and before i could speak the line went dead

i know damn well this bitch just hung up on me like that

oh hell noooo!!!!!

but something told me to call alex so i did

*ring*ring*ring*

a deep raspy voice picks up

"Hello betzy" alex saids calmly

"have you spoken to Mauricio like at all?" i ask him

"no but i can't stop thinking about fucking Aurora like she's been stained in my mind like since dinner" alex saids and i pause and think for a minute

"and why is that alex mhmm" i say and i hear him laugh

"well because i don't know maybe because i miss her it's been years since i lasted spoken or saw her"alex saids proudly

"mhm well okay bye alex"

i hang up

and now i need to talk to my brother

so i grab my keys and leave my house and drive to his house

and i have a spare key to his house and i unlock the door

and the house was quiet

"Helloo mauriicioo" i yell out loud

Nothing

"MAURICIOOOO ANSWER ME BITCH" i yell again but still no response

i run up the stairs and run into his bedroom but he wasn't in there i checked the closet NO i checked his bathroom NOPE

he wasn't there i ran into his office still nowhere to be found

i looked everywhere and he's not here what the fuckk

i went into his office once again and call his closest friend

ACE

i dial his number and call it

*ring*ring*ring*ring*ring*

"hello" i sleep voice answers

"Psstt Ace" i say waiting for his slow ass to speak up

"whatt betzyyy!!"Ace gets impatient

"do you know where Mauricio is at right now" i ask ace

"yeaa why??"Ace ask confusedly

"well because i kinda needa know because he's kinda like my brother you know" i say with sarcasm

"he's at a big mission right now betzy he won't be back until a few days" Ace saids getting frustrated with me

"wait where is his mission at tho like ACE im not playing around tell me where he's at" i say worryingly

"fine...he's in Italy right now some shit went wrong i don't know exactly what went wrong but something did but that doesn't mean you interfere with any of the bullshit you got it betzy?" ace saids seriously

knowing me i can't make any promises HEHE......

"i guess" i say annoyingly

"why aren't with that hot Ceo bestfriend of yours anyway" Ace saids trying to be funny

"she's in PaRISS...." i say and then i hear a laugh

"ha funny to hear that because I'm in paris right now" Ace saids

"whatt!!" i say with a high pitche in my voice

"mhmm i might just go try and get me some of that while im here you know" Ace saids with a fake flirtatious voice

"ACEE she is not a slut who is just gonna let you fuck one night and let you leave the next morning" tell Ace angrily

"Woah señorita who said she was a slut" i ace saids offensively

"plus it's not like you would ever have a chance with her or lay a finger on her" i tell Ace

"mhmm wanna bet on that betzy hmm" Ace saids

"sure but don't get you're feeling hurt when she rejects you" i say while laughing

"okay well i must go look for princess Aurora now bye señorita" Ace saids as the line went dead

HAHA the idiot really thinks he gots a chance with Aurora

HAHA my own brother doesn't even got a chance with her and he's married to her....LMAOO

but i went home a called it a night and went to bed

---

hoped you enjoyed CHAPTER nine of his moonlight

i

will try and post more chapters it's just alots going on in my life so i need y'all to be a bit patient with me im trying to write as much as possible

but thank you all for the love and support i really appreciate all of you sm <333

and whose y'alls favorite character

AURORA

MAURICIO

BETZY

ACE

ALEX

KAI

LET ME KNOW:))

BYE MY LOVES<33

Chapter 8
a paris night

(please don't be a silent reader)

get ready for this chapter because its gonna get real hot in here;)

ALEX'S POV:

after betzy called and asked if I've talked to Mauricio at all

but i haven't spoken to him in a few days and im pretty sure he was mad about

the whole bar situation with Aurora

was he mad that i was holding the girl who really belonged to me and not him

I've never seen Mauricio act this way over a woman

but i had bigger plan's and it wasn't gonna be very pretty either

---

third person pov:

Aurora left the hotel and went to explore the rest of paris in a cream silk dress

with a white furry jacket

and she went outside and started walking around and taking pictures with her phone and she finally got close to the Eiffel Tower and stand there admiring it and taking pictures of it for memories

til she gets interrupted by a deep raspy voice talking behind her

Aurora's pov:

i stand there taking pictures of the Eiffel Tower than i hear a

deep raspy voice speak behind me "well look what we have here little miss Ceo in paris..." i turn around to see ACE

"let me me find out you are stalking me now" i say sarcastically with a smile

"hmm maybe" he saids standing right next to me with a smile

"so Aurora what's got you here in paris tonight" Ace asks with a curious look on his face "hmm just trying get away from work cause i haven't had much time to myself" i tell Ace as we both stare at the Eiffel Tower

it says quiet for a few seconds "and why are you knowing you are no longer ms. Knight anymore" Ace saids curious

"no one is gonna find out because there isn't a ring" i say showing my empty hand

he chuckles and shakes his head gently and runs his hand through his jet black hair "well i could see that but eventually you're gonna have to got to events with him you know that Right...?" Ace saids seriously

i look down knowing its gonna have to happen eventually

"yea that's true..." i sigh in disappointment and Ace nods his head "wait where even is Mauricio at right now" i ask Ace curiously

Ace looks at me for a second and looks away "he's actually in Italy right now because some business went wrong but i don't know exactly what went wrong" Ace saids calmly

"ohh..." i say quietly and Ace looks at me with a smile and i give him a smile in return

"it seems to me that you and Mauricio have a history together huh" Ace saids and i chuckles quietly "well indeed we do" i tell Ace and gives me a look for me to tell him how

"okay well it all started when we were kids i met betzy and Mauricio but betzy was a year younger than me and Mauricio well he was way older" i Say and Ace shakes his head encouraging me to keep on going

"and my father and lioñel used to be really great friends and thats when i used to go over to their house all the time and it was my get away..." i say calmly

and Ace jerks his head gently and turns his head and looks at me weirdly "what do you mean by you're get away...?" Ace asks concerned

and i sigh in frustration "my dad was extremely Abusive to me and my siblings for the longest and one time he beat the living shit out of me that i had managed to get to the caraliño house and they saw how my father treated me and they took me and my sisters in for 3 years and my father's mafia went to war with mr. caraliño's mafia" i say coldly

and Ace looks away and i watch as he clenches his jaw and i could see the anger in his eyes

"you didn't deserve any of that" Ace saids softly and i just nod my head gently "yeah and sometimes i would wake up in the middle of the night to get a glass of water and Mauricio would be awake and would always ask me to come to his room and listen to him play his electric guitar and sometimes we would stay awake so long that i would wake up to him holding me in his arms and i was like 8 or 9 and he was like 16 or 17 i honestly forgot it's been so long" i tell Ace

and Ace shakes his head all crazy and looks at me weirdly once again "Waitt how old are you..?"Ace saids very curiously

and i start laughing "im 20 about to be 21" i tell Ace who goes into shock "so you still like a baby what the hell" Ace saids still in shock and i just nod my head

"when's you're birthday" Ace ask and i say "it's march the 13th" and he nods his head

"is it you're first time in Paris" Ace said calmly and i nod my head "come on I'll show you around princess Aurora" and reaches his hand out and i take his hand

and he starts walking and i follow him and he finally stops at the cute little restaurant

and we ate there and we went to explore more of Paris and he said he was a faster runner than me and next thing you know

im running down a alley with him running behind me

and running and laughing was all we were doing

and i keep on running down the alleyways til i hear silence

i stop running thinking he gave up i start walking back til im slammed against a wall and i see Beautiful Ace himself towered over me having me blocked by his arms side by side of me

"Hmm...you're so gorgeous" was all Ace said til he smashed his lips into mine

and he pulled away but something was telling me to kiss him back

so i smashed my lips into his our kiss was passionate

he held my waist pulling me closer to him and i move my arms around his neck

and we both pull away slowly and he moves the strands of my hair away from my face and smiles at me

"let's go back to my hotel okay hermosa" Ace saids and gently giving me a kiss and i just nod my head

and he takes my hand gently and walks with me

and eventually we make it to the lobby of the hotel

"woah this a very beautiful place..." i tell Ace and i hear him chuckle "well thank you i designed it all my self" Ace saids with that charming smile of his

"wait this is you're hotel" i ask him in excitement and he nods his head while laughing

his dimples<333

we get on the elevator and we walk into a luxurious hallway and he grabs my hand and leads me to his hotel room

and we walk and i look around admiring it

til we make a stop and Ace let's go of my hand and he grab his key and he opens the door for me and i slowly walk in and see a beautiful kitchen and living room that had to French doors with a beautiful balcony

i loved it

til i feel Ace taking off my jacket and i slowly walk to the balcony and i stop at the railing of the balcony and look at the Eiffel Tower

and a few moments later i feel wet kisses on my shoulder up to my neck

i couldn't help my moan it felt so wrong yet so right at the same time

and i turn around and stare into his beautiful green eyes and he leans in and kisses me

we got heated quick and he picked me up and i wrapped my legs around his waist and he just keeps kissing me while walking into his bedroom

and he makes it into his room and lays me down gently and hovers over me

and he continues to kiss me and i tug at his white dress shirt and he stops and unbutton his shirt and revealing his abs and he smiles at me staring at his abs

"like what you see love" Ace saids seductively and i stay quiet

and he slowly reaches his hand out to me and i take his hand and he sits me up and slowly lifts up my dress

and his eyes darken when it's only revealing me with white lace panties and no bra

he slowly lays me back down and hovers back over me and kisses my lips and starts going down leaving wet kisses all over my body til he starts pulling my panties down i felt like I was going crazy

this man has gave me a feeling that felt so good

he pulls them off and throws them somewhere

and he gently kisses my inner thighs and he kisses my clit and

then he started going crazy

and next thing you know it

I'm a moaning mess

he was pounding himself into and god we went at it for hours

til i hear my phone ring and he was still in me and i see that it was

Betzy calling so i picked up while still getting fucked like crazy

"heyy Auroraa!!" betzy saids happily

"h-heyy ahhh" i accidentally moan at loud and i hear betzy gasps

"Aurora what was thatt!!!" betzy saids curiously

"i-its nothi- ahh Acee" i moan out loud and completely forgetting betzy could hear me

"WHAT THE FUUUCKKK" i hear betzy yell out loud

and she hangs up and me and Ace stop and I sit up embarrassed about what just happened

what if betzy tell Mauricio im fucking Ace oh shitt

and Ace rubs my back and he pulls me into his arms and runs is hand through my hair and kisses my forehead

and i drift off to sleep in safe warm arms

---

hope you enjoyed chapter ten for his moonlight

but who is your favorite character

Aurora

Mauricio

Betzy

Ace

Kai

Alex

and how do y'all feel about this chapter ???

And Thank you for all the love and support i really appreciate it and hope y'all have a wonderful day or night:)))

Chapter 9
the truth

(please don't be a silent reader)

Maurico's pov:

when i get to Italy i start to think about Aurora and all the bad memories that we left behind here

this place is like hell itself

my dad called me and notified me that i need to bring back up just in case something else goes wrong

i was working with mr. diaz one of my dads bestfriends that was like an uncle to me since a very young age

we were sitting in the backseat of the car with mr. diaz who's name is Carlos

"so how's that arranged marriage going for ya so far nephew" Carlos saids and i turn my head towards him "it's been strange.." i tell Carlos who looks at me funny

"why is it strange nephew" Carlos asks looking at me still

"i don't know maybe because she's like one of the biggest CEOs in America" i say with my eyebrows rise up and carlos eyes widen and he looks away and chuckles "are you talking about Aurora selen knight" Carlos saids with a shocking look on his face

and i just nod my head at him and he looks away in disbelief

"i see why that is strange because she's literally a woman who wouldn't even look you're way" carlos saids while laughing

i mean he wasn't totally wrong but damn okay carlos

"but how did the two of you even get into the arranged marriage" Carlos asks confusingly

"her dad used to be the leader of the Mexican mafia down here in Italy" i tell him calmly

and Carlos remains silent for a few minutes til he broke the silence "wait is her father name antonio knight..?" Carlos asked

"yes sir that's his name" i say annoyingly

"ohh shit..." Carlos saids and a few minutes and we have arrived to our mission

the next day

i just got done with some business and now im headed back home thank god

while I'm on my private jet i fall asleep

a few hours later i was wakened by my uncle telling me we are back home

i get up and told my uncle goodbye and went home

after i arrived home everything was fine til betzy barged into my house all crazy

while i was trying to watch vampire diaries and betzy runs into my living and looks nervous

"Whaatt betzyyy" i say and she sits down on the couch and plays with her fingers

shit she's scared because she only does that when she's scared or nervous

"what's wrong angel" i ask betzy who was still sitting there

"soo....uhh are you aware that Ace and Aurora are Both in Paris right now" betzy saids fast

"no why....?" i say carelessly and she frowns at me "well you don't think it's a bit strange to you" betzy saids with a concern look on her face

"no betzy that's not any of my business and why are you even telling me this stuff in the first place" i tell her getting irritated by the questions

"ohh nooo reasonnn...." betzy saids with a fake smile and gets up and just leaves the house

what the fuck just happened

hmm Ace and Aurora in paris well how suspicious is that

oh it's honestly whatever at this point

---

third person pov:

Aurora was still sound asleep on Ace who was there just holding her in his sleep

but Ace manged to wake up before Aurora and do something nice for her for when she wakes up

he called hotel service to get breakfast and called some people to plan stuff out and everything he bought a beautiful Black silky dress for Aurora and beautiful earrings and a matching necklace

and Ace realized Aurora was still naked so he call his assistant kendal to get some clothes for Aurora to wear during the day

and by the time everything was ready Aurora started shifting in her sleep causing her to wake up

---

Aurora's pov:

i start shifting in my sleep which caused me to wake up and i see a beautiful sunrise from the window and i turn to my right to see Ace gone

i sat up and covering myself with the covers because i had nothing on

til i see Ace walk in and starts walking towards me and i start to get nervous

"hello my love how did you sleep.." Ace asks softly and soothingly as he makes eye contact with me

"i slept good" i tell Ace who just smiles "and how did you sleep" i asks softly and quietly

"i slept amazing knowing i got to hold a gorgeous girl last night" Ace saids while moving my hair put of my face and softly kisses me

and starts to stroking my cheek and i hold the covers tight on to me making sure he didn't see anything "love it's okay i already seen you're beautiful body" he saids softly with his deep raspy voice

"and here's this bag of clothes i got for you because i know you only came here with a dress and i wanted you to feel more comfortable since it's a bit cold outside today" he saids slowly putting the nice looking bag in front of me

"thank you Ace" i say quietly and he turns his face away and i he him whisper under his breath "fuuck" and i give him a concern look

"did i say something wrong" i ask and he turns his head back towards me "noo not at all i just love the way you say my name" Ace saids who smiles

"uh oh okay" i say with a confused tone in my voice

"here's the bathroom and i get out and let you change okay my love" he saids and once again kisses me and i just nod my head

and watch him walk out and close the door behind him

and i get up and take the sheet with me to the bathroom and the bag of clothes with me and closed the bathroom door

and i looked inside the black luxurious bag and see a black turtleneck with high waisted jeans and black high heel boots

well whoever picked this out must have good taste in clothing

i changed into the clothes and walk out the bathroom and walk in the living room and see Ace

leaning against the wall looking outside the window and turns his head towards me and slowly walking my way

and he finally approaches me and strokes my cheek and his charming smile starts to appear on his face revealing his dimples

"god you're so fucking beautiful" was all Ace saids and took my hand and lead me to the balcony and his hotel room

and i see the small beautiful circled table with two glasses of champagne and bacon and eggs and pancakes and macaroons on the table that looked absolutely delicious and i stare for a few seconds and i turn to see Ace who is laughing at my reaction to the table of food

"do you like it my love?" Ace saids with that fucking handsome ass smile of his

"i love it but you seriously didnt have to do this you know that right..?" i say with a frown on my face

and he makes a fake offensive face and put his hand on his chest where his hearts at "uhh of course i had to i mean baby look at you...you're absolutely perfect so yes i had too..." Ace saids with his deep raspy voice

"there's no such thing as perfect people it's a over used word" i say giving Ace attitude as we sit down

and Ace's eyes darken "don't make me throw you over my shoulder and have you begging for me like i did last night" Ace saids calmly

i just sit there smirking at what he just said

and i start to eat and so does Ace

after that we went out for more exploring in paris

and Ace insisted that he wants to spoil me and take me on a shopping spree

and he ended up taking away my credit card because i kept trying to pay for my own stuff

and we went back to my hotel and put my stuff there

and he said we wanted to go to dinner tonight and he showed me a beautiful black silky black dress

and i put it on and we left to go to dinner

we get into the back seat of the car as his driver drove us

and i look at the window and all a sudden i feel a big warm hand on my thigh and i look down at his veiny hand on my thigh

and he starts to rub my thigh

i just stare at his hand

and eventually we get to the restaurant and we get to our table and we start to talk more and getting to know about each other

til he stops talking "i got you something else baby" and he leans down and grabs a huge thing of bouquet of red roses

the red roses

i look at how huge the roses are and my eye's widen

and i see Ace chuckling at me

"do you like them hermosa" Ace said and i nod my head

and i realized something different about the restaurant

it's super quiet in here but when we got here it was loud

what the fuck

i look around and see nobody inside and i turn back to look at Ace who was smirking at me

"where did everyone go Ace..." i ask

"well i rented the whole restaurant out for just the two of us" Ace said confidently

and i just hum at him and we get our food and eat then got back into the car and half the car ride it was silent

and he kept his hand on my upper thigh the whole time

"i had a wonderful time with you hermosa" Ace saids looking at me with his sleepy eyes and tired voice

"i had a wonderful time with you too" i say quietly with a smile and he smiles back at me

and we make a stop and we were at my hotel and i was about to open my door til Ace slaps my hand gently and gets out the car and comes to my side and opens the door for me to get out

and he grabs my hand and helps me get out

and walks me to my hotel room door "well i guess this is a goodbye til next time amor" Ace saids sadly

"yup until next time Ace and thank you for a amazing time for my first time in paris after years of not being here" i tell Ace with a smile

and he makes eye contact with me and smiles gently "anything for you my precious little innocent girl" he saids as he puts his finger under my chin and lifts up my head and give me a long passionate kiss

and he pulls away slowly "goodbye baby" Ace saids and walks away

and i unlock my hotel door and open the door and walk in the dark and walk to the bad and put my flowers on the bed and

walk back in living and turn the light switch on and walk into the kitchen and turn the light as well

"so you and Ace now huh?" i hear a familiar female voice say

and I turn around and see betzy sitting on the couch with her legs crossed

"betzy what are you doing here" i say pouring myself a glass of champagne

"well i should be the one asking you why are in paris with Ace del ray black hmm" betzy saids with a bitchy attitude "betzy why the fuck do you care anyway" i ask her as i roll my eyes in annoyance "because he's totally not my brother's best fucking friend since childhood Aurora" Betzy shouts

"Betzy just leave" i tell her coldly with no emotion in my face or voice

and she stops and stares at me with hurt eyes "what" she saids sadly

"you heard me now leave" i saids carelessly while taking a sip of my champagne "whyy" she saids

"because I'm tired of being bossed around like I'm some fucking child because I'm not" i say rudely

"Aurora quit being ridiculous" betzy argues back

"being ridiculous mhmm okay say what you want.." i say with a evil smirk on my face and laugh

"what's so fucking funny to you Aurora" betzy saids standing up

"how you can come in here and act like you are all big and bad but betzy deep down we both know whose the most fucked up one in here and its not you" i say with a evil quiet laugh

"and why the hell is that Aurora" betzy said crossing her arms with her eyebrows rise up

"because you weren't raised by a man who almost beat the living shit out of you like mines did and didn't force you to shoot a bullet at someone at only 5 years old" i say coldly and heartlessly

betzy stays quiet for a few seconds "Aurora don't you dare pull that fucking card on me bitch." betzy spits

"does it look like give two fucks cause i don't and i haven't for a long time Betzy and you know that already" i say with evil eyes and she gulps and she looks around and remains silent

"why Aurora are you treating me like this" betzy saids concern

"because you are the reason why im going back into a lifestyle i ran away from years ago and I've worked too hard to lose everything now" i say with just anger in my voice

"Aurora i didn't have a choice i-"betzy saids but i cut her off

"yeah i know Ace told me all of it you knew and kept the word hidden just to save a man how could you" i say angry and hurt

"Aurora ple-" Betzy tries to finish her sentence but i cut her off

"you know it's funny to me how my own bestfriend keeps a huge secret from me and literally backstabs me and now I was forced to marry her older brother whose the devil himself....it's like those books" i say being sarcastic and bitchy

"Aurora STOOOP" betzy yells

and i look at her all crazy

"please....i don't want to fight anymore" betzy saids holding back her tears

"okay fine but just leave" i say pointing at the door

and i watch her leave

and i went straight to bed

Thank you for reading CHAPTER 11 of his moonlight

i hope you enjoyed

and thank you all for the love i appreciate it sm<333

(hope you have a good day or night)<33

Chapter 10

emotions

(please don't be a silent reader)

Mauricio's Pov:

i woke up late from being awake all night long trying to make business happen

and struggling to sleep not getting over the fact betzy told me About Ace and Aurora both being in Paris

but honestly how did she even know that the two were in paris anyway

she's been in town and the odd part is i haven't even heard from Ace in close to 3 days

what the fuck

it was 4 Pm now and i haven't even got out of the bed

til i recieved a call from Ace

i pick it up "hey I'm outside i need to talk to you" Ace saids sounding to be serious "Okay I'm coming" i say to Ace "that's what she said" Ace said laughing "shut the fuck up" i say chuckling and hang up and i walk downstairs shirtless and make to the front door and open it to reveal Ace in his sweatpants and tank top with his black jacket

"get in dumbass" i say to Ace who just walks in

"so what do you want to talk About Ace" i say rubbing my tired eyes

"well it's About paris" All Ace saids i look at him "okay what about it"

i say making a pot of coffee for me and Ace "well i bumped into someone there" Ace saids leaning back against the counter and a few minutes later the coffee was ready and i pour us cups of coffee

and i just hand him a mug of coffee "okay and may i ask who you bumped into there" i ask Ace

"well it was Aurora" Ace saids calmly with a smile on his face

"why are you smiling Ace" i ask curiously and Ace looks at me "well she told me About you and her when y'all were younger" Ace saids

and i burn my mouth at what he just said "Shit Mauricio are you good!" Ace saids

"no im okay just was shocked to hear that" i tell Ace who's laughing at me "what else did she tell you" i ask trying not to show fear

"well that was really all but that's not what i came to talk to you About" Ace saids calmly yet serious "okay and what's that" i ask Ace

"well i ended up have sex with her" Ace said sounding guilty i take another sip of my coffee before i could say anything Ace interrupts

"look I'm sorry it just sorta happened" Ace saids

"I'm not mad at you Ace...but i guess im willing to share her with only you tho" i tell Ace who's eyes widen at my responds

til i see a upset betzy walking towards Ace with a knife in her hand "woah betzy what the fuck are you doing" i yell out

"I'm going to fucking ki-" someone stops Betzy from her sentence "betzy seriously stop" i hear a soft calming voice saids

i move slightly away so i could get a better view at who said that

just for me to see the beautiful woman besides betzy Aurora

she stands there looking stress with betzy "no Aurora i will not let Ace do my brother like that or you!" betzy argues back with Aurora

and Aurora just sigh while putting her head down trying to keep her patients with betzy

"look Aurora i just care alot im sorry about last night" betzy saids apologetically and Aurora looks up looks around for a second

"it's okay betzy it's not you're fault in fact it was both of our faults we were both stress at that moment" Aurora saids with that beautiful smile that could lit up to the room

betzy gives Aurora a hug and Aurora gives one back

"so ladies what brings the both of you here today hmm..?" i ask the girls

"totally not me coming to kill Ace noOoo.....not at All..." betzy sarcastically so i think

Aurora just stays quiet and doesn't dare to look me in the eye but i was glad she didn't

but it pissed me off because she wouldn't looking at me at all

did she know i knew about Paris or is she just very shy

"well i-i think i should get going i don't want bother y'all" i hear Aurora's calmly Angelic voice saids

"Noo darling you are not bothering anyone stay..." i tell her and she turns around slowly

"ooh okayy.." she saids awkwardly which was quite cute

it's crazy how she hasn't changed much

i wanted to get her alone i wanted to talk to her for some reason I missed her

she was the only girl i showed my affection to besides betzy

i watch her walk to one of the kitchen stools and sit down next to betzy

betzy texted me and told me to go put a shirt on because she said Aurora finds that attractive and is nervous to look at me

i walk away and put a shirt on and came back to see no sign of betzy

Ace pointed towards the back door of the backyard

i walk outside and see betzy sitting on the patio with her arms crossed

"betzy what the hell is wrong with you now" i ask annoyingly

"nothing i heard what you told Ace....are you really gonna do that are you serious Mauricio"

"well i don't know the girl enough to run what she can or cannot do!" tell betzy who stays quiet

"and for the one who kept her a secret from me for years and you know how much i missed her" i tell betzy who looked ready to throw a punch any second "because Mauricio i know what you would have done if i told you she was still in my life" betzy argues back

"did mom and dad know about her being in you're life still" i ask curiously

"yes....they did" betzy saids sounding guilty

i don't say anything

"I'm sorry Mauricio but i was just trying to keep her safe she's my bestfriend" betzy said with the sound of hurt in her voice

"it's okay angel I'm not mad i understand you were just looking out for her" i tell her

"but did you tell her about her having to move in with me soon" i ask before she could say anything else

"nope but im about to right noow!" betzy saids running inside

what the fuck

i go running after her and find her already talking to Ace and Aurora

"well Aurora i have to tell you something and you're not gonna like this" betzy saids innocently

"uhh a-and what iiss that" Aurora saids nervously

"well you know that you and Mauricio are now in a arranged marriage and that one of the rules for that is having to live together in order to make it more believable.." betzy saids sounding professional kinda

"wait what..?" Aurora saids kinda frighten at what betzy just told her "well Aurora you have to understand that has to happen in every arranged marriage...im sorry" betzy tells Aurora

who is kinda in shocked and Ace tries and comfort her

she starts to freak out and her breathing started to become very unstable and Ace was holding onto her so she could calm down

and nothing was working and betzy was standing there trying to process what the hell was going on

and Aurora starts to calm down and Ace slowly lets go of her and she just grabs her keys and walks off

but nobody stops her from leaving this time

"What the fuck have i done" betzy saids looking up frustratingly

Aurora's pov:

i walk to my gtr and storm off and i needed to rethink life at the moment

i was angry and i never wanted this life and i ran away from my father to get Away from the mafia itself

i wasn't ready to be married im only 20 im still learning life by the minute and being married to a fucking stranger was not already a good look on me

and if people find out that I'm married to a fucking mafia leader

i could possibly ruin everything i worked so hard for

i was driving so fast that at this point i don't even value my life right now

my phone started blowing up by betzy and Ace i wasn't going to pick up

i simply put my phone on silent

i was headed to my hide out spot which was out on a mountain with a beautiful view of the city

and the sun was just setting i park my car and grab the left over alcohol i had in my car

i grab it and start thinking about everything and how i deserve all the bad shit happening to me and most likely more coming my way

knowing that i will have to live with a person who is the total opposite of me and lives a different lifestyle than me

i know it's not gonna be easy but i been through worst sadly...

after a while from drinking alot i needed to get home like right now

I'm shit faced right now

i get in my car slightly tumbling

i start the car and start driving everything was going well til

everything goes black.....

Hope you enjoy this CHAPTER

and if i forgot to mention the names are based on real people in my life but anyways

thank you for reading his moonlight

see ya next chapter love ya

Chapter 11
switched emotions

Betzy's pov:

after finally finding Aurora driving while being drunk i had to hack in a system to get her car to stop

and it wasn't easy but i was able to get it done

Mauricio and Ace went and got Aurora from out of the car and took her back to Mauricio's house

and i demanded that Mauricio take her to the guest bedroom

and Mauricio notified me that he had a mafia ball to attend to and Aurora had to be right by his side tonight

so i did what any bestfriend does for her bestfriend i went and picked out a dress for Aurora

and it was a dress i been dying to buy for her but she isn't much of a dress girl but today she was going to have to be

i went to one of the boutiques and i walked around and i see Alex who was standing looking at suits and some other shit

and he must have felt eyes on him because he turned his head towards me and started walking towards me "well it's not surprising to find you here" Alex saids thinking it was funny

"well it's surprising to find you here" i say annoyingly

"who you buying this beautiful tight dark green dress for...hmm" Alex saids curiously and i look at him with a bitchy look on my face

"For Aurora" i say trying not to strangle him to death right now

"hmmm that would look sexy on her" Alex saids with more of a seductive tone in his voice

"hey watch you're fucking mouth now Alex before i make you!!" i tell alex who goes in shocked at what i said to him

"well damn betzy my bad" Alex saids offensively and i just stare at him with evil eyes

"well i got to get this dress to someone important now bye" i tell Alex with a bitchy tone

and walk off and i didn't reget a damn thing i said or did cause why would i

i pay for the dress and leave and head back to Mauricio's house

as i was driving i recieve a text from Kai

Kai:

hey hermosa what are you up to rn

Betzy

nothing driving back to my brother's house to give my bestfriend a dress she will need for tonight

Kai

mhm are you going to be attending with her?

Betzy

yeah i kinda have to but are you going aswell

Kai

yeah im just wondering if you would like to go with me?

Betzy

omfg of course I will go with you!!!

Kai

okay hermosa i will see you tonight i love you.

---

i turned off my phone smiling at what kai asked me

but i need to focus on my bestfriend right now

a few minutes later

i finally arrived to Mauricio's house and parked my car and got the dress out and headed back into his house

and i saw Aurora sitting in the living on the couch with her legs crossed on the couch with a cup of probably coffee or tea in it

she was watching riverdale

this girl

she looked stressed out and she looked so fragile it made me frown at her and

she finally looked at me and her eyes go right back to the screen ignoring my existence

"aurora please say something please" i say with hurt in my voice hoping that she would have spoken or something

but once again she ignored me and the pain in my heart knowing she's upset and this could have been my fault the room felt 2 times more colder then it did when i came into the room

i got the chills but i walked out the room and tried to not cry or show any emotions for that matter

i was walking upstairs and into the hallway til I see Ace standing there leaning against the wall on his phone doing something that i personally didn't care to worry about honestly

and i just walk right past him

"hey betzy what's wrong" i hear Concern ace's voice say and i slowly turn back towards him

"Aurora is upset with me" i say quickly and ace looks down at the floor

"well betzy i could see why she would be" Ace saids calmly but damn that asshole is too straight up

"but im not saying it's because of you but what im saying is she's had alot of stress on her recently" Ace said trying to not be rude

"yeah i guess so" i say being dry

"well i need to get ready but can you go and give this to Aurora and let her know to start getting ready for tonight" i ask ace nicely and he gives a nod and grabs the dress from me and walks away

i walk away and try to find Mauricio and talk to him

after a few minutes of trying to search for the man he was in his office sitting down looking outside the window

and i lean against the doorframe and knock gently on the door

"come in" was all Mauricio said

i walk in and approach his desk and i let out a sigh hoping that would catch his attention and indeed worked

he slowly turns spins his chair back towards me and stares at me with a blank expression on his face

"what betzy" Mauricio saids carelessly

"how long is this ball going to be" i ask curiously and Mauricio lets out a sigh of frustration

"it's from six to eight thirty" Mauricio saids while grabbing his pen and started writing on something

i just walk away upset and i just wanted to get the day over with already

Aurora's pov

i wake up with a massive headache and feeling nauseated

i relize that I'm not in my bedroom but how

i don't even remember getting here what the fuck!

i get up and walk into the bathroom and look at myself in the mirror and looking like a whole ass trainwreck

lord have mercy

i turn the sink on and i wash my face to help me wake up more and not much of a trainwreck

after i washed my face i walked out the bathroom and walking back into bedroom looking at the luxurious room i couldn't tell where i was exactly

so i walked towards the double doors slowly and quietly and i gently turn the door knobs and open the doors successfully and walked into a long dimmed luxurious hallway as i make my way down it i see a staircase and i start sprinting down the hallway trying to get the fuck out of here

but then i come to a stop and taking a minute to process where im at

it looks very familiar like i been up here before

but as soon as I'm about to run again i hear footsteps approach behind me and i slowly look at who this person was to see Ace staring at me with smirk on his face

that brought me the chills

"what are you doing" is all ace saids to me still staring down at me waiting for my response

"I'm leaving" i say with a confused look on my face

"well it's too late Aurora" Ace saids calmly

but what is that supposed to mean by its too late

"too late for what ace?" i say confusingly

"betzy and Mauricio took all your belongings from all your houses and brought it here in a another bedroom that's just for you" Ace said coldly with zero emotion on his face

"haha Ace you got some jokes don't cha" i say with a smile thinking he was putting on a funny prank on me or something

"what's so funny Aurora im being so deadass with you" ace said seriously

"what?" i say back with a blank expression on my face

"come" Ace saids grabbing my hand and taking down the hallway and making a right and down another hallway and we approach a door and ace swings it open and i see a huge bedroom filled with all my belongings in it like my bed comforter, my vanity, makeup,and a bookshelf filled with books i own, my big tv, and my pillows, my everything in there

i don't say a word i just felt like I was being taken over and that my life has been stolen from me

i let go of ace's hand and walk inside looking around feeling weirded out by it all

"do you like it" i hear ace say and i slowly turn around and see ace leaning against the doorframe with his arms crossed and staring directly at me

"no" i say with a blank expression on my face "and why not?" ace said confusingly and i stare at him with evil eyes

i was mad i was hurt i was betrayed and i wasn't gonna let people step over me like this

"where's Mauricio" i say with a serious look on my face

"he's busy right now aurora" ace saids calmly

haha jokes on him i don't give a fuck if he's busy ohh im gonna talk to him whether he likes it or not

"i said where's Mauricio Ace" i say with a upset tone in my voice

"in his office damn" ace saids frustrated with me

and i nod my head and push ace to the side and went straight for Mauricio's office

as i start walking closer to it i hear ace yelling at me to come back but i didn't listen of course

i approach Mauricio's office door and swing it open carelessly to see Mauricio sitting there with his feet on his desk with his glasses on, shirtless with black sweatpants on

reading some paperwork of some kind

and his eyes shoot up to me

"yes Aurora how can i help you darling" Mauricio saids while still reading the paper

"i hate you so fucking much" i say upset with tears on the urge of falling down my face

"and why is that hmm?" Mauricio saids putting the paper down

"because you signed that contract not thinking about me and how i would feel" i say hurt with tears coming down my face

"oh Aurora baby don't cry be a big girl and get over it already damn" Mauricio saids being a total ass

"why me" i say looking at him who staring at me like im a damn dinner plate or something

"because why not?" Mauricio saids with a smirk on his face

i don't say anything but i just look down

til a few seconds later i feel fingers touch under my chin and lift the head up forcing me to look up to see Mauricio staring at her

"today i need you to put on the beautiful most fake ass act for the ball that you will be attending with me tonight as my wife" Mauricio saids with a fake pouting look on his face

i don't say anything i wanted to say something but nothing could come out

"okay Mi niña bonita" Mauricio saids with his deep raspy Spanish accent

i knew if i kept on fighting back with him it wasn't gonna get any better than this

i nod my head and slowly walking back

i went downstairs and started making me some nice cup of coffee to hopefully calm me down

after i made my coffee i went for the living room and sat down with turned on the tv

after awhile i hear someone walk in i knew it was betzy

so when she walked in i just ignored her presence as if she wasn't there at all

and she walked away after trying to get me to speak

and a few minutes later i see ace leaning against the wall staring at me holding a dark green dress

that was wrapped in clear plastic and ace starts walking towards me and sets the dress down and stands right in front of me as im sitting down on the couch

i look up at him and give him a weak smile

and ace opens his arms as if he was encouraging me to get up and hug him

"come on aurora" ace said with his arms out and with that charming smile of his

i stand up and slowly hug him and we stay like that for a few minutes

til he slowly pulls away

and looks down at me "well it's about time to get ready for tonight okay" ace saids grabbing the dress and handing me it and walks away i shrug my shoulders and start walking upstairs to my so called bedroom

and i reach the bedroom and walk into the bathroom and quickly slip out of my clothes and change into the beautiful dress

and i mean don't get me wrong betzy knows me too well and literally is like my sister so

she nailed it!

but i realized that the back of the dress had a zipper in the back

she i grabbed my phone and dialed betzy's number

*Ring*Ring*

she picks up and i hear her sigh on the other side of the phone

"betzy" i say quietly and softly

"yes aurora" i hear betzy says in a annoyed tone

"do you mind helping me with this zipper on the back of my dress" i say quietly and nicely as possible

and i hear betzy let out a sigh "mhmm yea sure im coming" betzy saids and the line went dead

i put the phone down and i wait for betzy to get to my room

and i see betzy behind me with a smile

and she walks more behind me and she pushes my hair gently to my shoulder and zips up the dress and she backs away and looks at me through the big mirror and smiles

"you look so beautiful" betzy saids with her classic high pitch voice

and i laugh out to her tone of voice

"thank you" i say quietly

and we share a laugh together

that when we get interrupted by ace yelling downstairs "are y'all ladies ready"

betzy scream out loud "yesss.." and she grabs my wrist and leads me out the bathroom

Betzy's dress

Aurora's dress

we walk down the hallway and betzy goes down the stairs first

and i wait for her to walk down first and as im about to go down i didn't realize that Mauricio and ace were both at the end of the stairs as if they were waiting for me to get down

as i walk down the stairs i can feel eyes on me

and i knew whose exact eyes that were on me

Mauricio.

i finally approached them

Mauricio dosen't hesitate to grab me by my waist and pull me beside him

which straddle me and i turn to look at betzy

to only see her looking our direction with her jaw dropped

i roll my eyes at her and hold in my laugh at betzy who was dumbfounded

Mauricio and ace look at each other and Mauricio hands were still placed on my waist and he starts walking but leading me with him and outside the house

i see a very nice limousine right outside the house

i watched betzy and ace get in and Mauricio stands there waiting for me to get in so i get in and Mauricio gets in after me and shuts the car door and immediately gets on his phone and starts typing away

and ace just looks out the car window and mean while betzy is just looking happy

for some reason

and me well i was just tired, confused, and annoyed by everything and everyone

but 10 minutes in i feel cold metal meet with my thigh and i flinch at the coldness of the metal touching my skin and the heavy warm hand

and i look down to see Mauricio's veiny tatted hand that was on my thigh and i look at his direction to see him scrolling through his phone with his other hand

while his left hand was relaxed onto my thigh

i didn't say anything just felt a bit weirded out at the fact his hand was just laying there and him still reminding unbothered by his hand being on my thigh

but not too long after we arrived to the luxurious building

What do you think happened after that?

i also wanna say how sorry i am for not giving the update that i said i would for three months

but i been very busy and haven't really had time but that doesn't mean i do write sometimes

i do write when i have the time too and i also wanna say have much i appreciate all of y'all for the love and support that y'all have been putting on my book and idk where i would be without any of you guys

and i love reading the comments they are my favorite parts of my day really and i will probably have another chapter coming very soon

but byyeeeee guys love yall and be safe my loves<333

CPSIA information can be obtained
at www.ICGtesting.com
Printed in the USA
LVHW031204310123
738241LV00013B/1531

9 781805 090120